the O in HOPE

ILLUSTRATED BY

Luci Shaw　　**Ned Bustard**

ivp
Kids

InterVarsity Press
P.O. Box 1400, Downers Grove, IL 60515-1426
ivpress.com • email@ivpress.com

*InterVarsity Press® is the book-publishing division of InterVarsity
Christian Fellowship/USA®, a movement of students and faculty active on campus at
hundreds of universities, colleges, and schools of nursing in the United States of America,
and a member movement of the International Fellowship of Evangelical Students.
For information about local and regional activities, visit intervarsity.org.*

*Text adapted from Luci Shaw, "The O in Hope,"
The Generosity, Paraclete Press, 2020.
Used with permission.*

Cover and Interior design: Ned Bustard

ISBN 978-1-5140-0265-0 (print)
ISBN 978-1-5140-0266-7 (digital)

Printed in China

Library of Congress Cataloging-in-Publication Data
A catalog record for this book is available from the Library of Congress.

P 21 20 19 18 17 16 15 14 13 12 11 10 9 8 7 6 5 4 3 2 1

Y 37 36 35 34 33 32 31 30 29 28 27 26 25 24 23 22 21

Some O things
to look for in this book:
orangutan, oar, oranges,
okapi, otter, oak, ox,
ocean, owl, ostrich,
and octopus

Hope holds one lovely vowel like a promise!

O is the
shape **o**f
a m**o**uth
singing,
and in the
col**o**r **o**f
a r**o**und,
red cherry.

"**O**h!"
say **o**ur
open eyes
at surprising
beauty,
and then,
"W**o**w!"

O is as c**o**mplete as
a wedding ring,

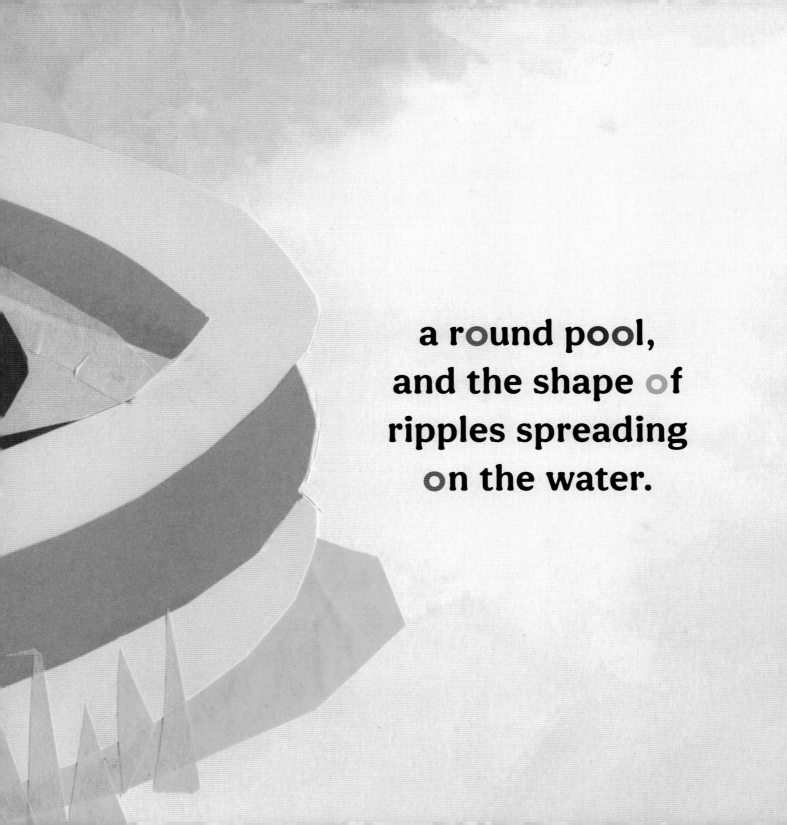

a round pool,
and the shape of
ripples spreading
on the water.

O is the
heart **of** l**o**ve,
and j**o**y.

O was in the invention of the wheel.

O multiplies
in the z**oo**,
in an **o**pen d**oo**r,

and in a
c**oo**l drink
on a h**o**t day.

O grows
in the heart
of a green
w**oo**d.

O is like
the m**o**o**n,
and the
l**o**o**ping
paths **o**f
planets.

You'll
find O
in food,
and
books,

and cotton socks, and useful tools, and knitting wool.

We love
the double O
in good,

and how
O is in itself
complete,
and whole.

Love forms
a circle
that holds
us all
together,

safe in
the center
of the
loving
heart of
GOD.

A Note from the Author

Writing this poem was one of my most enjoyable experiences! Words with the letter *o* in them arrived so easily, and the phrases and ideas developed organically. And then another halcyon surprise: out of the blue Ned Bustard sent me a series of vivid, ingenious images inspired by the poem. When some joyful words of mine elicit that kind of an enthusiastic artistic response, I'm convinced that God is in it from the beginning!

Poetry helps us treasure and value the diversity of creation, but it also teaches us to explore and appreciate the joy of language. And because poetry condenses ideas with its compact phrases, this means that each word evokes an image—a mental picture. Reading a poem aloud enhances this experience. No poem is meant to remain silent on the printed page, so reading it with children and then linking words with the illustrations is intended to excite and enrich, with the double gift of beauty and meaning.

Younger children will delight in their search for the colorful *o*'s in the text, but my deep desire is that this book (the words *and* the illustrations) gives you an opportunity to discuss the true meaning of *hope*. We live in a world that is dim on hope, but our faith reminds us of the true source of our hope—God's love and grace—and has introduced us to "a better hope" (Hebrews 7:19).

After exploring this book's words and pictures together, I hope you continue the conversation:

- How does the poem makes you feel?
- What is your favorite illustration? Why?
- What are some things—little things or big things—you hope for?

And if this book inspires children to write their own poem or story, or create some art, both Ned and I would be so very pleased!

May you be abundantly blessed with love, joy, peace, and hope.

Luci Shaw

Let us hold unswervingly to the hope we profess,
for he who promised is faithful.

Hebrews 10:23